The Velvet Cloak

LOOK OUT FOR MORE OF

Amber's Dressing-Up Dreams

The Velvet
Cloak

JENNY OLDFIELD

Hodder
Children's
Books

A division of Hachette Children's Books

A Catalogue record for this book is available from the British Library

ISBN-13: 978 0 340 95595 6

Printed and bound in Great Britain
by Clays Ltd, St Ives plc

The paper and board used in this paperback by Hodder Children's
Books are natural recyclable products made from wood grown
insustainable forests. The manufacturing processes conform to the
environmental regulations of the country of origin.

Hodder Children's Books
A division of Hachette Children's Books
338 Euston Rd, London NW1 3BH
An Hachette Livre UK company

"I'm going to a fancy dress party but I don't know what to wear," Pearl told Amber and Lily.

"Come and look in my dressing-up box," Amber suggested.

The three girls ran down to Amber's basement.

"Where's the satin dress?" Lily asked Amber. "You know – the pretty pink one that you wore before."

"And the princess tiara?" Pearl added.

"Oh, those old things!" Amber was trying to forget the magic twirls and dazzle that had swept her into a dream world. "Here, Pearl – try this fairy costume. It was a Christmas present from my gran."

Pearl tried on the white frilly dress. She turned on the spot. "It's creased," she said. "I'd like something sparkly, with sequins and stuff."

"You're not expecting much!" Amber said, rummaging deep in the box. She came up with her mum's old party dress.

"Pink sequins!" Lily grabbed the dress and held it up against Pearl. "Cool!"

Pearl tried it on while Amber rummaged

6

again. This time she came up with a dusty black cloak.

"Yuck, that's whiffy!" Lily told her. "Throw it away!"

But Amber had other ideas. She wrapped the cloak around her. "I'm the Wicked Witch of the West!" she cackled.

"Get lost, Amber!" Pearl cried. The pink sequins suited her. She'd found her perfect dress.

"I'm the wicked witch!" Amber chanted, raising her arms and spinning round.

A cloud of dust rose from the cloak. It began to glitter gold and silver.

"Stop, Amber, you're choking us!" Lily coughed.

Amber kept on spinning. Lily's voice faded. There was a dazzling light.

7

Oh no, not again! Amber thought as she spun out of her basement and into a dream.

"Oh no, not again!" Pearl gasped, staring at the empty spot where Amber had twirled.

"Amber, Pearl, Lily – where are you?" Amber's mum called from the top of the basement stairs!

"Quick!" Lily groaned. "Think of an excuse!"

Pearl shrugged. "'Er, sorry, Amber's mum – Amber dressed up in an old black cloak then she vanished.'"

"Not the truth, silly!" Lily panicked. "Amber's definitely up to something and she's not letting us in on it."

"When she comes back, we have to make her tell," Pearl decided, doing a pink sequin twirl.

"*If*," Lily insisted. "*If* Amber comes back . . ."

"Amber?" Amber's mum came slowly down the stairs.

"We're out of here!" Pearl and Lily decided, fleeing through the French doors into the garden.

2

It serves me right for showing off! Miserably Amber sat down by a dying fire. She was back in the Cinderella cellar, with its tall cupboards and the pumpkin on the bare table. Upstairs she could hear the Ugly Sisters shrieking and fighting.

I should never have dressed up in this old cloak, she told herself. *I should have thrown it away, like Lily said!*

11

"Cinderella, it's time to curl my hair!" Louisa yelled.

"Polish my toenails!" Charlotte wailed.

"Lazy, good-for-nothing girl!" the sisters bellowed. "Come upstairs this minute. We need you to help us get ready for the Ball!"

"What took you so long?" Charlotte demanded.

Amber had taken her time, trudging upstairs and along the grand corridor. Now she stuffed wedges of cotton wool between Charlotte's toes then opened a small bottle of red varnish.

"Leave that. Curl my hair!" Louisa ordered.

"Polish!" Charlotte spat.

"Curl!" Louisa shrieked.

Their mother, Octavia, appeared at the bedroom door. "Girls, girls!" she protested. "The whole street can hear you."

"It's Cinderella's fault," Louisa whined. "She's a lazy, useless girl!"

Yeah, where did I hear that before? Amber sighed to herself. Nothing had improved since her last visit to Cinderella world. If anything, Charlotte and Louisa had got worse.

"Mother, we have less than four hours to get ready for the Prince's Ball," Charlotte complained. "Cinderella's fingers are too clumsy, she moves too slowly. You must take her away and punish her."

Much worse! Amber groaned.

"No! Make her curl my hair and then pull the laces of my bodice tighter still!"

Louisa demanded. "Tell her to make me so beautiful that the Prince will fall in love with me at first glance!"

"No chance!" Amber said under her breath. She shrank back as Octavia strode towards her.

"Tonight you will have no supper!" Octavia hissed. Her dark, glittering eyes were cruel. "You will be locked in the cellar while Charlotte and Louisa go to the Ball."

Amber spoke out. "I don't care. I'm not scared of you!"

But she remembered last time, how the shadowy stranger had crept into the house to kidnap her. She had yelled and fought, but the Uglies had sat on her and squished her, and no one had come to her aid.

Octavia's evil eyes narrowed with anger. "This time you will be taught a lesson you will never forget!"

"Go ahead," Amber muttered, turning away and trying to look braver than she felt.

I'm stuck again! she thought.

"Ouch!" Louisa cried as Amber wound her hair into tight curls. She seized the

hairbrush and whacked her on the arm.

"Ouch!" Amber frowned then tugged a little harder at Louisa's locks.

Alone and helpless. Stuck, with no way out.

As Amber brushed and curled, she prepared herself for the worst.

Here's where I – Cinderella – get chucked in the cellar with the mice and cobwebs while Louisa, Charlotte and their evil mum go to the Palace and party!

Trumpets played. Town-criers cried.

"Oh yez! Oh yez! His Highness, Prince Charming, invites all his people to a Grand Ball!"

Dah-dah-da-daah! The trumpets blared.

"Tonight. At the Palace! There will be music and song!"

Dah-daah!

"Charlotte, where did you put our

invitation?" Louisa cried. She searched on her sister's dressing-table, knocking aside bottles of perfume and a fluffy powder puff.

Down in the street, the Prince's men read their master's proclamation.

"Cinderella, where is our invitation?" Charlotte turned on Amber. She flew into a temper, seizing Amber's hair and tugging hard.

"I never touched it!" This was mad, Amber thought. The whole town was going crazy over one silly party.

"Every subject is invited to the Palace!" the town-crier called. "From the highest in the land to the lowest boot-boy in the street!"

Oh yeah, what happened to Buttons? Amber wondered as Louisa grabbed hold of her skirt and ripped it out of spite.

Buttons the boot-boy was the only person Amber rated in this crazy place. He kept popping up and helping her when she least expected him.

"His Grace, the Duke of Zapotania will be there, with the beauteous Countess of Sylvaria!"

"The Countess of Sylvaria!" Charlotte let Amber go then rushed to the window. "What is the colour of the Countess's dress?" she shrieked at the town-crier. "Will it clash with my pale lilac gown?"

"The Duke of Zapotania!" Louisa sighed, sinking down on to the bed. "Next to the Prince, he is the most handsome man alive!"

*

There were three hours to go and a hundred and one things for Amber still to do.

She dashed along corridors, carrying stiff lace petticoats, searching for ribbons, hair-clips and white kid gloves.

"More powder for my face!" Charlotte cried as she discovered a pimple on her cheek.

"Oh Lord, I hate the colour of this dress!" Louisa wailed, staring into the mirror. "Cinderella, it's your fault. You know I suit apple green better than peach pink!"

Too late! Amber thought with a secret grin.

"Powder!" Charlotte demanded again.

So Amber ran down the corridor to

Octavia's empty room, where she found a dish of white powder.

As she headed back to Charlotte's bedroom, she collided headlong with her hopeless old dad.

Or rather, Cinderella's doddery father.

"Cinders, my dear!" The old man looked over the rim of his glasses. He seemed upset. "It saddens me that you cannot go to the Prince's Ball."

"It's OK. I don't mind," Amber hastily replied.

"So, despite Octavia's wishes, I have decided that you must go with your step-sisters. You deserve to have some fun, my child."

"It's not my kind of thing. Honest."

Her father shook his head and drew

Amber into the library where he spent most of his time. He sat her down in a chair by the long window then looked her up and down. "First of all, we must find you a party dress," he realised.

"No, really," Amber mumbled. She tried to hide the rips in her ragged red skirt.

The old man stared at his shabby daughter. "And we must wash your face and curl your lovely golden hair."

"I don't want to go to the Ball," Amber tried to tell him. "And Octavia doesn't want me to go either, or Charlotte and Louisa for that matter."

"Why not?"

Amber shrugged. "I guess they're jealous."

Her father was shocked. "Cinderella,

you're mistaken," he argued. "Octavia would not stoop to such feelings."

Want to bet? Amber decided it was time to put the old man straight about his wicked wife. "Believe me, she would. She even tried to have me kidnapped!"

"Surely you're mistaken," her old dad sighed.

"No, I was carried off into the forest," Amber insisted. "And, get this – Octavia already got rid of three husbands. You're her fourth!"

"Tut-tut-tut!" He shook his head.

Amber was in way too far to back out. "It's true. Buttons told me the whole story."

"It can't be true!" the old man stammered.

"You'd better believe it!" Amber argued.

"I don't understand. Why do you put up with her and the Uglies? They're always fighting and nagging. They spend all your money on dresses and tiaras!"

"I married Octavia and made a solemn promise to take care of her," he reminded Amber. "For better or worse. For richer, for poorer."

Make that "poorer"! Amber thought. Soon the old man would have nothing left. "I'm trying to help," she sighed. But she saw it was hopeless.

Her father only stroked her hair and sighed. He sat at his desk and opened a large, leather-bound book.

"Can I go now?" Amber asked. At a sad nod from him, she slipped out of the room and quietly closed the door.

4

"Not so fast!" Octavia had been lurking in the corridor. She grabbed Amber and lifted her clean off her feet. "I heard every word!"

Amber kicked and wriggled. "So punish me!" she yelled. "See if I care!"

Octavia carried Amber kicking and wriggling to the cellar. She pushed her down the stone steps. "You were trying to turn the old fool against me," she scoffed. "But you will never succeed."

Amber sat with a bump on the cellar floor. "I expect you're going to tell me why not," she muttered.

Octavia's dress rustled as she gathered her wide skirt and turned on the narrow steps. "Because he is kind and honest," she sneered. "And a man with a good heart, such as your father, will not recognise wickedness, though it stares him in the face!"

Amber felt down in the dumps, realising that the wicked stepmother had a point.

"Cinderella, are you there?" a voice hissed.

She'd been locked in the cellar for at

least half an hour. In her mind's eye she couldn't get rid of Octavia's mean face and glittering eyes.

"Buttons, is that you?" She ran upstairs and put her ear to the door.

"Right first time!"

"You don't know how glad I am to hear your voice!"

There was a short pause. "Steady on, girl!" Buttons protested. "I've gone red as a beetroot out here!"

"This is serious, Buttons! Listen, Octavia locked me in!"

"So what's new?" Every time Buttons visited the house on an errand, Cinderella was locked in the cellar, or else being kidnapped. "Hey, you should see those two sisters up there in their rooms – ribbons and lace everywhere, tiaras on crooked, hair all over the place. It's chaos."

"Good!" Amber grunted. "Buttons, can you do something for me?"

"What?"

"Can you try and get hold of the key to this door?"

There was another pause and then a cry and a scuffle.

After what seemed like an age, Buttons came back. "Sorry, Cinders, but that was Octavia," he reported breathlessly. "The tigress pounced and gave me a proper mauling!"

"What for?" Amber wanted to know.

"For talking to you through this door, if you must know. But I snuck back as soon as I could."

"Thanks, Buttons!"

"And the answer to your question is – no, I can't get you the key. It's dangling from the chain around Octavia's neck, and I don't know a man in this country brave enough to snatch it from her!"

Amber nodded then sighed.

"Are you still there?" Buttons asked.

"Where else would I be?"

"Are you crying?"

"No!"

"I bet you are, Cinders – blubbing 'cos you can't get dressed up in your party frock to go to the Prince's Ball like every other girl in town."

"I am *not* crying!" Amber hissed through the thick door. "I don't care about the stupid Ball. And I don't even have a party dress. I just want to get out of here before it's too late!"

The minutes ticked by. Footsteps tip-tapped down the hallway. Amber heard Charlotte screech Buttons' name. "Go to the flower shop at once!" she ordered. "Bring me a posy of purple lilacs!"

"Yes, miss. Right away."

"And don't tell Louisa!" Charlotte hissed.

Tip-tap, tip-tap. Charlotte went away. Then – *scuff-scuff* – Buttons slouched off down the hall.

Amber felt the silence of the cellar settle on her. She shivered. *OK, so no key!* she thought. *But there has to be another way out of here!*

She looked around the dark room, hearing the scuttle of mice-feet inside a cupboard. She brushed against cobwebs as she searched in every shadowy corner.

Mice and spiders, just like before. No secret doors or boarded windows. No way out.

Amber sat heavily on the stool by the empty grate. She stared at the ashes.

"Cind-er-ella, loo-ook up!" a spooky voice said.

Amber jumped a mile. She knocked over the stool and stumbled against the wall.

"I said, look up, Cinders!"

The muffled voice came from high inside the fireplace. Amber took a deep breath and edged forward. She peered up the tall, narrow chimney.

"Are you a g-g-ghost?" she whispered.

"Yes, the ghost of King Henry the Eighth. Whoo-ooo!"

"Buttons!" Amber said crossly. "What are you doing up on the roof?"

"Waiting for you to climb up the chimney and join me," came the reply.

"You're joking!" she gasped. "You expect me to squeeze all the way up there?"

"Why not?" Buttons' voice seemed a long way off.

"Because I hate heights!" Craning her neck, Amber could see a circle of daylight, plus the dark outline of Buttons' head.

"I thought you wanted to get out," he hissed. "What are you waiting for?"

"I can't . . . I mean . . . I've never . . ." Amber's heart thudded, her hands went clammy with fear. "Buttons, I can't do it!"

"Course you can!" came the scornful reply. "Any ragged little chimney sweep could scramble up and down here in no time!"

"I'm not a chimney sweep. I don't know how."

"Well now's the time to learn," Buttons insisted. "Are you coming or not?"

5

Swiftly Amber made a decision and hitched up her skirt. She wrapped the black cloak around her. "Wait there for me," she pleaded with Buttons.

"I would if I could," he replied. "But I reckon I've been spotted by Tom the footman. Yep, he's yelling for me to come down. Looks like it's time for me to vanish!"

"Don't go!" Amber begged. She wanted Buttons' friendly face to greet her at the top.

But he disappeared, and so it was up to her to make the dark climb alone.

"So far so good!" she muttered as she found her first foothold. She felt with her fingertips, edging her way up the sooty chimney stack.

"Don't look down," she muttered to herself. "Look up at the daylight!"

Slowly she climbed. Soot fell on her face, loose bricks wobbled, but she was almost there.

"I have to keep going!" Amber insisted, her heart banging loudly against her ribs.

"Yuck!" The chimney stack grew narrower and she had to squeeze through

the last few metres, holding her breath and shoving herself upwards.

Then at last her head poked out of the top. She could see the grey, sloping rooftops and the blue sky. She could breathe again.

"I'm free!" Amber whispered, emerging from the chimney. She shook soot from her cloak. It blew away in the wind.

"Whoa!" she cried. The wind caught her

and blew her sideways. She tried to grab hold of the tall chimney stack, but her feet slipped on the smooth slates.

"Help!" Amber cried.

She slipped down the steep roof, gathering speed.

The blue sky seemed to tilt and turn. Amber clutched with her fingertips, but nothing could stop her from falling.

She reached the edge of the roof. She glimpsed the busy street way below. Then, with a shrill scream, she tumbled down.

"Sit her up!"

"Splash her face!"

"Slap her – she'll soon come round!"

Faint voices floated around Amber's aching head. She tried to open her eyes.

"At least she's still breathing!" she heard someone say.

"Uh-uh-ugh!" Amber moaned.

"Stand back and give her some air." One voice took control.

"Where am I?" Amber moaned as she opened her eyes at last. A circle of dirty faces stared down at her.

"She wants to know where she is!" the main voice crowed. It belonged to a boy with a thin face and spiky red hair.

Slowly Amber managed to focus. "Who are you?"

The skinny boy stuck his thumbs under the lapels of his ragged jacket then puffed out his chest. "She wants to know who I am!"

"Don't tell me she doesn't recognise you,

Spike!" another boy laughed. "Everyone knows your ugly mug!"

Not me! Amber thought. She sat up stiffly. "What exactly happened?"

Spike grinned down at her with a mouthful of crooked teeth. "What *exactly* happened was – you were careless. You fell from a roof and knocked yourself out. But don't worry, we were there to catch you!"

"I fell!" Amber gasped, recalling the terrible moment. She looked round at the strange faces. "What happened to Buttons?"

"You mean the boot-boy?" Spike asked. "He got nabbed by the footman and hauled off by the redcoats, Lord knows where!"

"I don't understand." As Amber struggled to her feet, she felt shaky and bruised. "Why would you rescue me?"

Spike winked then grinned. "Come now. There's no need to play Little Miss Innocent with us, Cinderella."

"I'm not Cinder— Oh, forget it!" Amber

decided that this scruffy gang would never believe the full story. She looked anxiously round the dingy room. "Just tell me where I am," she pleaded.

Spike ignored her. "That was quite a bang on the head you took back there, Cinders. Luckily, me, Jem here, and Sally – we shoved a cartload of hay in your way and broke your fall. Otherwise . . ."

". . . Otherwise you'd have snapped your neck like a stick of celery," the girl called Sally grinned cheerfully.

"Anyhow, no sooner did you land smack in the middle of the hay than we three charged off with the hand-cart and brought you down the back alleys, out of the way of the redcoats," Jem explained.

Sally nodded. "They'd have nabbed

you, like they nabbed the boot-boy. And we always look after our own when we see them in a jam."

"A jam?" Amber stared at the ragged gang.

"A pickle. A spot of bother." Spike got to the point. "We wouldn't want to see a girl like you landing in gaol, would we? No, we pickpockets stick together!"

"Pickpockets!" Amber gasped.

"Lord love us, she ain't a girl, she's a blooming parrot!" Jem broke in. "'A jam? Pickpockets!' – Pretty Polly!"

"I'm not a pick—" Amber began.

"Course you're not!" Spike said with a cheeky wink.

"I am not!"

"No – you're an angel! Just like me,

standing here polishing my halo!"

At this, the rest of the gang fell about laughing.

"Polishing 'is 'alo!" Jem echoed.

Suddenly Spike raised his hand and they fell silent. "The point is, Cinders, we saved your bacon."

"Yes. Thank you!" Amber said breathlessly. Though things hadn't gone quite to plan, she was at least free from Octavia and the Uglies.

Spike jumped back in. "So you owe us a favour."

Amber nodded. "Definitely. Anything you like," she promised rashly.

"Good girl!" Spike grinned. He sat Amber down on a wobbly wooden chair which he pulled from a dark corner. "Now, you know what night this is, don't you?"

Amber frowned. Her mind was still fuzzy. "Er – Saturday?"

"Oh, Miss Angel!" Jem laughed. "Little Miss Butter-wouldn't-melt!"

Spike got to the point once more, circling Amber as he spoke. "Saturday yes. But it's also the day of the Prince's Ball, ain't it?"

Jem, Sally and the others nodded happily.

"The best night of the year. You know what I mean?" Spike winked and came to a stop a few centimetres from Amber's puzzled face.

When Amber shook her head it hurt. "Ouch!" she moaned.

"The night when everyone gets dressed

48

up in their silks and satins."

"Booti-ful!" Sally swooned.

"The ladies put on their pearl necklaces and diamond rings. The gentlemen wear their best pocket-watches, dangling from fancy gold chains."

"El-e-gant!" Jem sighed.

Amber stared from one to the other. *Uh-oh!* she thought.

"Ah, now the penny's beginning to drop!" Spike said. "You see where I'm heading, don't you, Cinders?"

Amber frowned and shook her head.

Spike took her hand and patted it. "There, there. Diamonds and pearls, dripping from the ladies and gents as they go up the Palace steps. That's what makes it a special night for thieves like us!"

"I can't – I won't!" she gasped.

Spike's hand tightened round her wrist. "No such word as 'Can't', Cinderella."

"No such word!" the others echoed.

Spike came closer still and his look was suddenly cruel. "You can't fool me – those dainty fingers were made for picking pockets."

"No!" Amber pleaded.

But Spike held her tight. "Yes, my girl," he insisted coldly. "This is how you pay us back for saving your bacon."

"Saving your bacon!" Sally and Jem said softly.

Spike smiled triumphantly. "You come thieving with us, Cinderella, and help us pick the pockets of the richest in the land!"

6

"First of all, we have to clean you up."
Taking Amber out into a back yard,
Sally poured a bucket of water over
Amber's head.

"Hey, that's f-f-freezing!" Amber
shivered.

"We've got to make you respectable,"
Sally insisted. "We can't have you going
out with us looking like a beggar!"

Amber glanced round the yard. It was surrounded by high brick walls.

"Don't even think about it," Sally said quickly.

"What do you mean?" Amber wiped her face with the rough towel Sally had given her.

"Don't think about running off. Spike would only chase after you and drag you back kicking and screaming. It ain't worth it. Believe me – I know!"

Wisely Amber took Sally at her word. She let her drag a comb through her tangled hair. "How long have you been in Spike's gang?" she asked.

"Since I was a babe in arms and my mother dumped me down a back alley to starve or freeze to death,

whichever came first."

"That's horrible!" Amber was shocked. Now she looked more closely, she saw that Sally was skin and bone. Her blue dress was loose, her light brown hair hung like rats' tails and her grey eyes were dull and lifeless.

"It happens," Sally shrugged. Before she

led Amber back inside, she paused for one last piece of advice. "Now, Cinders, if you're a clever girl and know what's good for you, you'll do a nice, neat job for Spike at the Palace tonight, and he'll let you off lightly."

"Meaning what?" Amber asked.

"Meaning, he'll take from you any items of jewellery, fine lace, or gold chains that you snatch from the party guests, then he'll send you quietly on your way."

"And if I don't?" Amber asked, her voice quivering. "What then?"

Sally leaned close and whispered in Amber's ear. "Spike has a nasty temper, believe me."

Amber gasped and drew back, but Sally held her fast.

"He's wicked if you anger him," Sally warned. "Ask Jem. He has the scars to prove it!"

"Well done, Sally – Cinders scrubs up good." Sitting at a bare table with his gang, Spike was handing out orders for the night.

Amber frowned and tried to melt into the background.

"Jem, you choose two to take with you to the High Street. There'll be rich pickings among the party guests getting ready to walk up the hill to the Palace."

Jem nodded and slipped out of the thieves' den with two companions.

"Snug, you go to the Palace gates with Sal. I'll take Cinders down to the Old

Bridge, see what we can find there. We'll all meet back here in an hour."

"Good luck!" Sally said to Amber with a wink. She left quickly with a round-faced, dark-haired boy who looked no more than six or seven.

"Now, Cinders, it's time to see how good you are at picking pockets!" Spike grinned and hauled Amber out into a dark alleyway. He led the way through a maze of twisting passages, down steps, round corners until they came to a bridge.

"I'm no good at all!" she protested, trying to hang back. "Useless. Believe me!"

"Chin up," he told her, dragging her on. "Try to fit in – look as if you're enjoying yourself!"

Emerging from the shadows, Amber strolled with Spike into a crowd of happy people.

"The Prince has lit the riverside with a thousand lanterns!" A mother pointed out the chain of glowing lights to her small child.

"His servants carry flaming torches to lead guests up the steps to the Palace." An ancient man sat by the bridge, watching the celebrations. "I remember the old days, when the Prince's grandfather married his young bride. The town was lit up, just the same!"

Amber heard coach wheels rattle over cobbled streets. She turned and glimpsed a fine lady inside the coach.

"Make way for the Countess of

Sylvaria!" the coachman called.

"Perfect!" Spike hissed at Amber. "She'll be dripping with jewels, this one. Come on, Cinders, it's time to do your stuff!"

Instead of making way, he stepped boldly in front of the coach and waved it to a halt. "Hold it. Your horse is lame," he cried to the coachman. "It looks pretty bad to me!"

The countess poked her head out of the window. She wore a headdress of tall purple feathers and a gown of matching silk. A diamond necklace sparkled around her neck. "Drive on!" she told the coachman crossly.

Amber stared but didn't move.

"What are you waiting for?" Spike muttered. "Grab the necklace!"

The diamonds glittered in the torchlight. Amber held her breath. *I won't!* she said to herself.

Just then another coach rattled full speed towards them. "Make way for the Duchess of Pravio!" the second coachman cried.

"Grab the necklace!" Spike shouted at Amber over the din.

A blonde, bejewelled head poked out of the second coach. "Trust the stupid Sylvaria woman to block our way!" the fur-clad Duchess yelled. "Don't stop, coachman. Drive on!"

Hey! Amber thought. *I'm here! Your horses are about to mow me down!*

Sure enough, the Duchess's coachman drove right on through the narrow gap.

Whoa! Amber threw herself to the ground and crawled under the Countess's coach. Huge wooden wheels rolled within centimetres of Amber's body. She put her arms over her head and prayed.

"Get up!" Spike reached under the coach. He dragged Amber to safety before

the Countess's coachman whipped his horses and drove on.

"What were you doing back there?" Spike demanded. He pulled Amber into the shadows, on to a quay that smelled of fish. "Why didn't you grab the necklace when I gave you the chance?"

Amber trembled. "I was trapped. They would've run me over!"

"Before that," Spike insisted. "You had all the time in the world. You could've reached up and snatched those jewels, easy as pie!"

Amber took a deep breath. She heard the dark water lap against the quay, saw the thousand glowing lights by the riverside. "I told you I wasn't a pickpocket," she muttered. "But you wouldn't listen to me."

Spike narrowed his eyes. "So how come you were leaving the big house by the chimney route?" he reminded her. "Honest girls don't climb chimneys to get out of a house – they generally leave by the front door."

"Ah!" How could she explain? *Octavia and the Uglies – they think I'm Cinderella and they want to get rid of me, but they're making a big mistake. I'm really Amber and nothing is what it seems . . .*

"Well?" Spike demanded, making a fist and thrusting it under Amber's chin. "Tell me the truth, Cinders, and make it good!"

7

Get me out of here! Amber was desperate. She looked round for her fusspot fairy godmother. *Come and wave your magic wand!*

"I'm still waiting!" Spike muttered.

Stars twinkled overhead, the dark water flowed softly by. *If I jump in this river, will I drown?* Amber wondered.

Spike's eyes glittered.

"OK, Spike, the thing is – this is all one huge mistake!" she began nervously.

He edged nearer.

"OK, OK. The roof thing – it was Buttons' idea. Octavia – my stepmother – wears the cellar key on a chain around her neck. Buttons said the only way out was up the chimney."

Spike grunted. "Go on."

"Octavia wants rid of me. I mean, seriously, she's already hired someone to kidnap me. And she's been rotten to me since the moment she married my old dad. And now she doesn't want me to get his money when he dies."

Spike nodded. He seemed willing to believe this part at least.

"So I had to escape. Besides, the Uglies

were getting on my nerves big time – dressing up in their fancy frocks. They think the Prince will fall in love with them, but they have no chance, believe me."

"How do you know?" Spike asked suspiciously.

Amber managed to meet his gaze. "I just do."

"OK, if they're ugly you're probably right. Go on."

"That's all," Amber insisted. "I had to nip out quick while they were busy getting ready for the Ball, and it was Buttons who suggested the chimney. Then he got nabbed by the soldiers."

Spike nodded. "We saw that."

"So you believe me?" Amber pleaded.

She wished the black water would open up and swallow her. Anything to get out of here.

"Maybe," Spike muttered. "Maybe not."

"It's true!" Amber insisted.

He shot her a suspicious glance. "And you haven't left anything out?"

Only the bit about the black cloak in my dressing-up box at home, and the shiny cloud of gold and silver. The magic stuff! Amber shook her head and looked away.

"So, say I believe you," Spike said rapidly. He'd spotted a boat decked out with a red and gold silk canopy heading towards the quay. Its flaming lights bobbed, the oars cut smoothly through the dark water. "That still leaves us with a problem."

"But you have to understand, I'm not a – erm – um . . ."

"A thief?" Spike shot back. He grabbed her wrist and pulled her away from the approaching boat. "Not a pickpocket like me, eh, Cinders?"

"Yes. No. I'm not!" His sharp words confused her. "Let me go!"

"Ah!" he laughed, cutting down a dark passage, out of sight of the boatman and a load of party guests all chattering excitedly about the Prince's Ball.

"When does it begin? . . . Are we late? . . . Hold my skirt clear of the mud . . . How long will it take us to walk to the Palace?"

Spike sighed and held on to Amber. "That's exactly the problem I'm talking about – this business of letting you go."

Amber tried to twist her wrist free.

"The thing is, Cinders – now you know about us," Spike explained. A beam of light flashed across the alley, lighting up his red, spiky hair.

"Hardly anything," Amber protested. "This all happened so quick. I'm confused!"

"You know where we live for a start. You know about Jem, Snug and Sally. You know about me."

"But I won't tell anyone!" Amber gasped. She heard footsteps coming up the steps, the rustle of silk skirts and the click of gentlemen's boots. "Honestly, Spike – I won't say a word!"

His grip on her wrist didn't slacken, even as the boatman swung his light down the alley and caught them both in its glare.

"Don't move!" the boatman ordered, then called for help. "Tell the redcoats to come quick," he yelled. "Here are two young villains up to no good, caught like rats in a trap!"

Spike and Amber were young and quick. The boatman was old.

By the time the call went out for redcoats to capture two no-good youngsters lurking by the water's edge, the quarry had disappeared.

"Over here!" Spike told Amber. He vaulted over a stack of empty baskets and led the way up yet another alley.

Amber followed. Behind her, she heard

the boatman blunder into the pile of baskets.

"This way!" Spike insisted, running along a wooden walkway overlooking the river.

Amber had no choice. As the boatman swore and kicked the baskets aside, she followed Spike until they were sure he could not follow them.

"I've an idea to teach the old fool to

mind his own business," Spike threatened, turning back.

"No!" This time it was Amber who led the way on to a brightly lit street. She felt Spike stick to her, close as her own shadow.

"There *is* still one way to solve our little problem," he began, as if their conversation had never been interrupted.

For a moment, Amber's hopes rose. "You can trust me," she insisted. "If you let me go, I won't breathe a word!"

Spike grimaced. "I never trusted anyone in my life, Cinders, and I'm not going to start with you."

Amber's hopes plummeted. "What then?"

"You see those two fine ladies across the street?" Spike pointed to a couple of girls dressed up for the Prince's Ball, mincing along the pavement in their satin shoes. One was dressed in pale lilac, the other in peach pink.

"That's the Uglies!" Amber gasped. "It's Charlotte and Louisa. They're on their way to the Palace."

"Exactly," Spike said with a sly grin. "All dressed up in their diamond tiaras!"

Amber stared at him, then at Charlotte and Louisa, heads held high, little heels going clickety-click.

"Now, Cinders, you know what I want you to do," Spike said steadily. "You have to steal those jewels from off their heads."

"But they'll recognise me!" Amber said, her heart hammering against her chest. "You can't be serious!"

"Cross my heart," Spike swore. He painted the full picture for a stunned, slow-witted Amber. "I'll be watching you every bit of the way. You snatch the jewels. They recognise you and scream your name fit to burst."

"But why?" Amber pleaded. "Do you want me to get caught?"

He shook his head. "No. You make your getaway quick as you can. With the jewels, of course. Bring them back to me in our den. Make sure no one follows you."

"And then what?" Amber asked, her head in a spin.

"And then you're one of us, like it or not," Spike sneered. "Just think about it, Cinders – you'll be a thief like me, a brand new member of the gang!"

8

"I am so-o-o excited!" Louisa fluttered her peach pink fan. She swept along the street in her grand ball gown.

"I can hardly breathe for excitement!" Charlotte agreed, grasping her bouquet of purple lilacs. "This is the thrilling-est night ever!"

The streets were bright and bustling. At the top of the hill the Prince's Palace was lit with a thousand golden lights.

"No messing this time!" Spike urged Amber.

She clenched her fists and swallowed hard. Crossing the street, she followed in the Uglies' footsteps.

"The Prince will ask me to dance, I'm sure of it," Louisa sighed. "The Countess of Sylvaria will not stand a chance!"

"He will notice me first," Charlotte argued. "I am so much taller and prettier than you, Louisa. I will stand out from the crowd."

Louisa closed her fan then flashed it open again. "That's *so* not true!" she muttered.

A few steps behind them, Amber gathered her long cloak about her. *I can't*

believe I'm doing this! she thought, sneaking a glance across the street at Spike.

"Louisa, walk a little way behind," Charlotte ordered. "Tell me if my petticoat shows below the hem of my gown."

"You forget, I am not your servant," Louisa snapped back. She strode ahead of her sister. "I am not Cinderella at your beck and call."

"Then I shan't tell you that your tiara is crooked," Charlotte retorted. She pushed her way through the happy crowd. "Or that your sash is undone."

Bickering as always, the sisters climbed the steps to the Palace.

Amber watched and heard them. She knew Spike was still in the shadows. *This time I have to go for it!* she thought, pulling her hood over her head and gaining ground.

"Tell me, is it still crooked?" Louisa fiddled with her tiara, which fell down over her forehead. "Oh, look what you made me do!"

Charlotte laughed and strode on up the steps. "I will have the first dance!" she vowed.

"Wait for me!" Louisa wailed.

It's now or never! Amber thought, keeping her head well down and stepping in front of Louisa. She reached out to snatch the crooked tiara.

"Get out of my way!" Louisa tutted, giving Amber a big shove.

Amber fell back down the steps,

dragging Louisa with her.

"Oh!" Louisa cried. "Oh! Oh! Oh!"

"Come along, Louisa!" Charlotte called impatiently.

The hood fell clear of Amber's face. Louisa stared her in the eye.

"Aagh!!" Louisa screeched. "Cinderella, what are you doing here?"

It all happened in a flash. Louisa recognised Amber and screamed. Charlotte came running down the steps.

"Get back to your cellar!" Louisa yelled, shoving Amber again. "You needn't think you're coming to the Ball with Charlotte and me, so there!"

This made Amber mad.

Otherwise I might never have gone ahead

and done it, she thought later. *It was Louisa and Charlotte being mean to me that made me snatch their tiaras.*

Louisa shoved and Amber fought back. Charlotte joined in. Amber was soon

buried under a froth of lilac and pink silk.

"Go back home, Cinderella!" Charlotte shouted. "You're dirty and horrid. The Prince doesn't want you at his Ball!"

Amber kicked and wriggled. She made a grab for Louisa's sparkling tiara and pulled it from her head.

"Ouch! Ooh! Ouch!" Louisa cried as her curls fell loose around her face.

"Little wretch!" Charlotte yelled, beating Amber over the head with her bouquet and dragging her up from the ground.

Amber ducked as Charlotte aimed another blow. Then she sprang up and made a second successful snatch.

Now Amber had two tiaras in her hands and two sisters shrieking into her face.

"Cinderella, give those to me!"

Charlotte cried. "Have you gone mad? Come back!"

But Amber was off, ducking again and dashing past the Uglies, stranded and gasping like fish out of water.

"Stop, thief!" Louisa screamed.

"Come back, Cinderella, or I'll tell Mama!" Charlotte cried.

There was no time to think. Amber grasped the tiaras and dashed on up the steps.

"Where are you off to? Come this way!" Spike hissed from down below.

Amber glanced round. There were hundreds of party-goers blocking the way. Charlotte and Louisa were screaming. No way was she turning back.

So, as Spike cut his losses and ran off, Amber dashed up the steps two at a time, past guests arriving early at the palace, up to the soldiers on duty at the great gates.

"Stop that thief!" the Uglies yelled,

setting the soldiers on Amber's trail.

One tried to block her way with his spear. Another stepped in front of her.

If I get caught with these tiaras, I've had it! Amber thought. *I'm never going to talk my way out of this one!*

So she did the only thing she could – she stamped hard on the first soldier's toe. As he doubled up and dropped his spear,

Amber aimed a kick at the second guard's shin. He dodged clear, but it gave her a split second to rush past him and through the gate into the Palace grounds.

Everything was ready for the Ball. Bright lanterns hung around the yard, red and gold flags fluttered around the edge of the tall fountain.

Amber saw maid-servants carrying trays of dainty cakes into the Palace, and men with silver cups and bottles of dark red liquid.

"Bring more wine!" a man with gold braid on his red uniform called. "Take it to the long gallery."

In front of the grand entrance to the Palace, two housemaids swept the crimson carpet free of the final specks of dust.

But Amber didn't have much time to take in the scene. She glanced behind her to see that the two soldiers were back on duty, with the Uglies yelling in their ears. They were pointing and looking her way.

Amber glanced down at the two glittering tiaras which she'd never wanted to steal in the first place, until the Uglies had made her mad. Now she wished she'd never done it. "I really, really want to get rid of these!" she said out loud.

But how?

"There!" Spotting two life-sized stone lions at either side of the entrance, Amber quickly perched the tiaras on their heads and dashed through the doors.

"After her!" Charlotte bawled.

"Don't let her get away!" Louisa shrieked.

9

Amber found herself in a grand hallway with marble stairs curving up to the first floor. There were portraits of kings and queens on the walls and statues everywhere.

At first there was no one around.

Amber heaved a sigh of relief and looked for a place to hide.

But then she heard footsteps marching

down the marble corridor.

"Is everything prepared?" a voice asked.

"Yes, Your Highness," came the reply. "The musicians are in their places in the long gallery, the banquet is ready."

"Very well, let us begin," Prince Charming said as he strode into view.

Amber gasped and shrank back. Outside the door, Charlotte and Louisa were still making a fuss about their stolen tiaras.

"Now the Prince will never notice us!" they wailed. "He will dance with the Countess of Sylvaria. Our chances are ruined!"

"Use your eyes – the tiaras are on the lions' heads!" Amber muttered.

The painted portraits stared severely down at her.

"OK, OK!" she shrugged. "So there's no need to tell me – I got *myself* into this mess!"

From the portrait at the top of the stairs, King Lidium the Third seemed to nod his crowned head.

"And I'll get myself out!" Amber hissed as Prince Charming and his servant steadily approached.

"Let the Ball begin!" Prince Charming declared.

Servants threw open the doors. Guests entered the Palace.

Don't move a muscle! Amber told herself. She took up position next to a statue of a long-dead prince. *Don't blink, try not to breathe!*

"Did you ever see a statue so lifelike?" a gentleman murmured as he passed close to Amber. "Your Highness, these works of art are wonderful!"

Prince Charming bowed and smiled as he greeted his guests.

It's working, Amber thought as she stared straight ahead. *They think I'm a statue!*

In the long gallery the music began.

"Ah, Countess!" Prince Charming stepped forward to meet his guest of honour.

The Countess of Sylvaria in glorious purple made a low curtsey. She fluttered her eyelashes and smiled sweetly.

Uh-oh, Prince C, don't fall for the girlie stuff! Amber said to herself. *The Countess is wrong for you. It'll never work out!*

And she had to admit that the Prince was totally fit, just like everybody said. He was tall and slim. He looked great in his dark blue velvet coat and white trousers.

The music played and the Prince took the Countess by the hand. He passed so close to Amber that she could have reached out and touched him.

Prince Charming glanced at her.

Amber stood perfectly still.

He looked again, seemed puzzled, then walked smoothly on.

As the crowd flowed into the marble hall and followed Prince Charming into the

long gallery, Amber relaxed and sank back into the shadows.

"Phew!" she murmured, tilting her head back and forth. "I'm stiff!"

"We're too late!" Charlotte cried as she and Louisa burst in through the door in a flurry of peach pink and lilac, still minus their diamond tiaras. Their hair was a mess, their faces were red and sweaty.

"We've missed the first dance!"

Amber quickly hid behind a tall statue.

"It's all Cinderella's fault!" Louisa moaned. "She didn't want us to dance with the Prince, the spiteful wretch!"

Together the sisters bustled through the hall towards the gallery.

Phew again. But OK, what now? Amber looked round and spotted a door under the grand staircase. She guessed that it led to the servants' quarters and decided it would be a good way to slip out unnoticed. But when she tried the door, it was locked.

There was nothing for it but to leave by the way she'd come.

Softly Amber tiptoed across the shiny floor. She reached the wide doors and peeped out into the courtyard. There were no soldiers in sight – only the fountain in the distance and the stone lions guarding the doors.

. . . And Spike leaning against a lion, twirling the Uglies' tiaras between his fingers.

"I 'ave to say it, Cinders – you're a big disappointment to me." Spike stood in Amber's way, twiddling the tiaras.

"Oh, help – not you again!" Amber murmured with a big sigh. She felt tears of disappointment well up and trickle down her cheeks.

Spike moved in on her. "You make the snatch then you chuck the gems away. What's the point of that?"

"Go away!" Amber pleaded. "I don't want to be a pickpocket. Leave me alone!" Tears fell with a plop on the stone cobbles.

Then, without warning, a warm wind blew. It made the flaming torches dance and flicker. Red sparks flew towards Amber and Spike.

A cloud of sparks fell on Spike and his

shabby jacket began to smoulder. He yelped, sprinted for the fountain and dived straight in.

Amber looked up at the fierce orange sparks. She waited for them to turn silver.

"Do not cry, Cinderella!" her fairy godmother said through the silver haze. "There is still time for you to go to the Ball!"

10

It was always the tears that did it. They brought the good fairy rushing to Amber's aid.

"Thanks for rescuing me from Spike," Amber began. "But about the Ball . . ."

Her fairy godmother twinkled and swished her wand. "Not now, dear, I'm busy doing magic," she said.

Swish-swish, sparkle, sparkle.

"I-don't-wanna-go!" Amber gabbled. She'd told her before, but the fairy never listened.

"First we must get you back home," Fairy G insisted.

Swish.

They were in the dingy Cinderella cellar. Amber was standing barefoot in her thin cotton petticoat.

"Now we must put on your dress and tiara."

Swish-swish. A silver light surrounded Amber. She looked down and saw she was wearing her beautiful pink satin dress decorated with pearls and pink ribbons.

"So pretty!" the fairy declared, reaching out to tweak Amber's sparkling diamond tiara. "Oh my dear, the Prince is certain to fall in love the moment he sees you!"

Amber shook her head.

"But you're not quite ready yet," Fairy G decided. "The night is cold. You need a soft velvet cloak to keep you warm."

"Believe me, I don't!" Amber protested weakly. But she knew she would get the magic cloak whether she wanted it or not.

And – *swish* – the fairy waved her wand one last time.

Witchy-woo! The dusty black cloak vanished and Amber was wearing a soft, warm, dark blue velvet one with a hood lined with silk and a collar studded with tiny diamonds shining like stars in the night sky.

"Perfect!" the fairy declared.

It was time for Amber to turn around

and see how the outfit felt – to turn full circle and then turn again, letting the cloak swing out, until a silver glitter lit up the cellar and she grew dizzy.

She closed her eyes.

"Here she is!" Pearl cried.

"At long last," Lily added, marching towards Amber.

Amber opened her eyes and saw her friends out in the garden. Pearl was wearing the pink sequin dress. Lily was looking cross.

"OK, Amber, tell us where you got the cloak." Lily came forward to touch the soft, dark velvet. "And no fibs this time!"

"Yeah, tell us the truth, Amber," Pearl insisted. "We're sick of the excuses you gave us about the dress and the tiara."

"Well . . ." Amber began, then hesitated.

"Well?" Lily and Pearl demanded.

"Well, there's this fairy godmother," she went on. "With a magic wand and everything."

"Where?" Lily asked, glancing round.

"I can't see her!" Pearl scoffed.

This was hard, but Amber was doing her best. "No. You have to find something magic in the dressing-up box first."

"Like that old black cloak you were wearing?" Pearl said.

"And the red skirt and the straw hat?" Lily asked.

"Exactly!" Amber nodded.

"Are you saying that the fairy waves her wand and turns them into this?" Lily felt the warm softness of Amber's blue velvet cloak.

Amber nodded. "It's magic!"

Lily and Pearl stared.

". . . No way!" Pearl said, flouncing off in her sequins.

". . . Are you serious?" Lily asked, open-mouthed.

Amber smiled and nodded. Then she shrugged. "But hey, no way did I expect you and Pearl to believe me – so let's go and have tea!"

Have you checked out...

www.dressingupdreams.net

It's the place to go for games, downloads, activities, sneak previews and lots of fun!

You'll find a special dressing-up game and lots of activities and fun things to do, as well as news on Dressing-Up Dreams and all your favourite characters.

Sign up to the newsletter at **www.dressingupdreams.net** to receive extra clothes for your Dressing-Up Dreams doll and the opportunity to enter special members only competitions.

What happens next...?
Log onto www.dressingupdreams.net for a sneak preview of my next adventure!